THE LOVE OF REINCARNATION

A TRUE LOVE STORY OF AN IAS OFFICER AND A SCHOOL TEACHER

ANAND KUMAR YADAV

ISBN 979-888591223-5

To true love

Contents

Acknowledgements

First, I praise the Universe for guiding me towards the purpose of my life.

Before I pay my gratitude else, I would like to thank my dear and lovely readers who bought my first book, read it and took the pain to connect with me. Thank you so much. It's your love and affection that motivated me to write this one.

Prologue

The story of life can be summarized in a few short words. It has never been ending.

We come into this universe for a few seconds, minutes, hours, days, months, or years. We all know that the soul does not dwell inside the body forever. Our soul disguises from one species to another species.

Sometimes, our reincarnation revives that we have lost something in our past birth. A picture comes into our mind and makes us curious to know our past existence.

When two souls are destined to be together, they meet anyway. We don't make any plan but it happens in the spur of the moment.

Indeed, reincarnation is a shade of our past birth. Sometimes, we live in the present past, or future. But our current situations belong to the shade of our reincarnation. It might be arduous to live without ups and downs in life.

Sometimes, reincarnation revives us beautiful moments of past birth and glimpses a light on our completed and uncompleted dreams.

Epigraph

Life is a natural phenomenon.

A drop of PURE LOVE contains an ocean of transformative power.

Love has no culture, boundaries, race, or religion. It is pure and beautiful like the early sunrise falling in the lake.

Introduction

Sometimes, he recalls his past birth. A dream depicts a scene from the past birth. He tries to escape from all those scenes which revive his past birth. He is curious to know all dreams which bring light to show him beloved.

Ankit belongs to an impoverished family and Anjali comes from an affluent family. Their love story begins in 10th standard but they are nescience about love. After 10th standard, they do not meet each other for 2 years, but he hopes to see her.

His parents cannot bear his study but somehow, he pursues his graduation. After graduation, he desires to become an IAS officer but he does not have enough money for accommodation and coaching fees.

Anjali pursues her graduation and she works as a government school teacher. She keeps a promise that she will never get married to anyone except him. But her parents opt for a final wedding date with someone else.

He strives towards his interview. His endeavors have gone rewarded. She commits suicide and tries to leave this peaceful universe forever.

He goes to celebrate his friend's wedding by own car but suddenly, they get an accident. He loses his parents, his beloved Anjali, and himself.

He gets rebirth on this planet and reincarnation revives his past birth.

CHAPTER ONE

Non-age

I am Ankit; I have died a few years ago in a car accident. The reincarnation depicts my memories. I do some brainstorming about dreams. I dispel my thoughts from memories, but an intimate relationship engages me. Although I jot this down without explicit information, I make a ceaseless effort to see obscure dreams.

I met my soulmate, Anjali. She was barely ten year's old genius, captivating, and effulgent girl in her school but she never heeded her face and beauty. She was from an affluent family background.

We were playing a game together on the school campus. She was running around a mango tree. Seven boys and girls were following her. She suddenly got into an accident with the pole and got an injury to her head. She collapsed on the earth and breathed hard. I tried to wake her many times but she was like a dead body. I pinched a few drops of water on her face but she did not awake. I started crying and could not understand what should I do.

I took her on a bicycle and went to the dispensary. I laid her on the bed. The doctor used antiseptic ointment, cotton strips, and medicines. She awoke and felt a little bit well. I dropped her home. I thought that her father will not be furious with me but he said; do not come to my home and do not go to school or anywhere with my daughter. I listen to everything very calmly and did not utter any word. I was scared that my body was trembling.

I was drastically crying coz I did not want to break our friendship. An infant thought born in my mind; I would be a superman and would fight with her father. I would defeat him and we would live together.

The next morning, we met her on the school campus and we did plenty of conversations with each other. We felt fresh wind carrying a beautiful fragrance circulated us.

Anjali, your father frightened me that we will never meet again at school, or outside school. He will be a villain in our movie. We are an actor and actresses; I said.

She started laughing at my meaningless joke. I saw a beautiful smile was flickering on her lips.

Your smile is gorgeous. You live in my heart, and that place is only for you; I said.

She stared at me and said; Ankit, you are a good boy. We can't be separated by any type of external or internal forces.

The next day, we did a pedestrian walk about 3 km. Finally, we reached school. I saw every student was doing morning prayer.

We were late so we were ready for castigation. Her legs were trembling.

Anjali, why do you have fear; I asked her.

My father will beat me and will disallow me to get an education if he will know that I go to school with you.

I hold her hand and encouraged her that nobody will let him know. We had been waiting for 10 minutes in front of the college gate. Finally, morning prayer had been finished. We took our seats in the classroom.

The principal called us into his cabin. He was a very strict teacher in the school. His face was like a furious monkey. He never used to talk politely with any student. He always used to stick for punishment. He raised his eyebrow and his speckle touched the end of his nose.

He asked; why did you both get late?

We were scared so we could not reply to anything. He pointed his finger towards me and said; Hey, I am asking you, why are you looking at her. You both will get punishment for coming late.

I was afraid that he will beat us with a stick. I wanted to speak lie him but my mouth had become a cube of ice. I saw her wet eyes which gave me the energy to convince him. I make courage inside my trembling body and said; Sir, she had been collapsed on the road. I held her hand and followed a petite step.

He felt our pain and emotion and saw fear inside our eyes. Thank God; he did not beat us by his stick.

I thought; he will only tell our parents that we had secured the first and second positions in the class but he wanted to give a surprise to our parents.

I had a lot of courage, attitude, and confidence coz I topped my school. I made my mind that her father will treat me as a brilliant student and will accept our friendship. But I did not know what will happen after facing him. I reached her home in the evening. She was washing pots, and vessels. I saw her father was taking a rest in the corridor. I saw his furious eyes which were staring at me.

Someone informed him that I went to school with Anjali. The principal punished us for being late in morning prayer.

You will never meet and go with her to school otherwise I will tell your parents; her father said.

Ok! Uncle.

I know that if my parents will know it then they will be sick or worry about my future. They were working hard for my future and were providing every facility for me like other students who were coming from a rich family. They have had a big dream that one day I will be successful in my life and will get their better treatment.

We were living in a small hut in a small town. I have had only a one-acre farm, which was an ancient property. My parents were working on the farm as our essential resource for liveliness.

She ignored me and did not enjoy my company. I tried to talk with her but she denied the conversation with me. Her friend told me that Ankit, her father had beaten her. If she will be with you or keep a conversation with you then he will not allow her to get an education. Please keep your distance from her otherwise she will lose a chance to get an education.

I held her hand and decided that we will not meet and will not keep the conversation again but it was hard to get separation from my beloved without any reason.

Our principal announced the parent's meeting. He wanted to meet with parents whose children secured a good position in the class.

The principal distributed awards to every student who secured first, second, and third positions in the class. He announced Anjali's name, her parents came to the stage and they felt proud of her.

The principal announced my name. I saw my parent's smile, which was flickering on their dry lips. They were scared, therefore; they were not coming on the stage with me. They were feeling abominable that they cannot speak any word if anyone ask something on the stage. I held their hand and got on stage.

What do you want to see in your son in the future? Principal asked.

I have a desire to see him as a police officer; my father replied.

Someone laughed at my parents and someone appreciated them. I could not understand why were people laughing at my father.

Dad, why are people laughing at you; I asked.

Beta, they think, we cannot further afford your study; he replied.

It's like a fire that produced energy inside my veins. I decided that I will be a police officer and will get treatment in a good hospital for my parents. I will buy a farm and will build our new home. I will give every facility to my parents.

I could not meet her even on the last day of school. I did not know where she will get admission to the next class. Everyone was spending his or her spare time at home or a relative's home.

I was living with my parents. We were poor so my relatives did not like us. They did not treat us well or respect us. Villagers were torching us. Our neighbors were dominating us. They wanted to show their money power and workforce, but my parents did not reply anything.

It is a crime to keep silent if someone making you trouble without any reason. You should raise your voice against those people who try to dominate you. It is a crime that you do not raise your voice against the worst people. It shows that you are a coward. Sometimes we are not able to raise our voice against them. Therefore, we keep silent and wait for a good time.

CHAPTER TWO

Separation

I got admission to a good government college. Someone told my father that your son is brilliant so you can get his admission to a private organization or good institute. My parents wanted to send me to a good college for a good education but they could not bear it. I stayed at home with my parents and helped them with farming work.

My draining eyes were looking at her shade but she was not coming in front of me. Sometimes, she used to come home but I could not meet with her. I was curious to know when she will come home. Her parents knew that she had been fallen in love with me, so they did not want to make any complications. They thought that she will make it complicated day by day, therefore he dropped her Nanihal.

Sometimes, she used to come home for one week during her vacation. It's have been a long to meet and talk to her. After a few months, I wrote a letter and passed it to Sarita.

My dear beloved ♥?Anjali.

I know you are doing well. One year has been passed. I tried many times to meet you but you always ignored me. I visited your home but you were not at your home.

I want to meet you at least once. I do not know what is happening to me. I am always missing you. You were my

Sunshine friend who can understand me.

I wanted to study in a good college but I did not get admission due to a financial crisis. I know you got admission to a good college. I visited your home your father told me that you have been migrated to your Nanihal.

I met with your friend Sarita. She has left her study because her parent was looking bridegroom for her. You know, everyone is getting married except for a few boys and girls. I wrote this letter to you whenever you will come home, she will give you, my letter. It depends on you whether you will meet me or not.

If you will meet me then tell your friend Sarita. She will inform me.

Your beloved Ankit?

I waited for three months but Sarita did not tell me anything. I hoped that she will come on this occasion of Maa Lakshmi puja.

The market was three km away from my home and five km away from her home. Sarita told me that Anjali wants to meet my family.

Where will we meet? I asked.

She will wait for you on the school campus.

Ok!

We will meet tomorrow.

Done; she replied.

The next day, I told my parents that we are going to meet my college friend, Anjali. My mother gave me Rs. 20, which was equal to 2000 for that day.

It took around 20 minutes to reach the school campus. I saw Anjali and Sarita were waiting for us. It had been taking a long time to meet her. Her wet eyes express her love. We both could not control our emotions so we cried and hugged.

Why did you cry? Is she your classmate? Did you not meet her after your 10th class? My father was throwing a series of questions. Yes, papa, she is my classmate, Anjali who secured first class in the 10th exam. You have been met her.

Beti, I know your father is rich in the village. I can speak with your parents if you don't have any objections. I will sell my home and farm for my son's happiness; my father said.

His sacrifices for my life always motivated me to achieve my dreams. They were ready to sacrifices everything for my happiness and dreams. I took them in my arms and tears poured from my eyes. She wiped my tears and held my hand.

We enjoyed ourselves a lot at the Deepawali festival. Anjali told me that Ankit, could we go to any restaurant. I nodded but I knew that I cannot afford it because I have had only Rs. 20. I did not want to make her insult so I did not want to eat at any restaurant.

Son let's go, what is wrong with you? Why are you not going?

I could not say anything but she was a brilliant girl, so Anjali understood my problem. She said; do not worry Ankit. It is a party from my side. She held my hand and pulled me.

We visited a good restaurant. She ordered a few delicious foods. After 20 minutes, we enjoyed delicious food. My parents were surprised; they never had have seen these delicious meals in their life. People were enjoying themselves with their family and a few couples were enjoying themselves for the moment. We finished our lunch and she paid the bill.

She purchased clothes for her parents. She bestowed a few clothes upon my parents but my parents did not want to accept this priceless gift.

Beti, why are you buying clothes for us? I cannot give you beside of your keepsake.

Uncle, it's from my heartiest side, so I don't need to take anything besides this present; she replied.

They could not express their deep emotion but we could feel them. Their emotion poured from their eyes. I saw pure love in their eyes.

I did not use Rs. 20. I saved it for my parent's medicine, so I bought medicine for them.

Anjali, when and how will we meet again? I asked.

Ankit, I will give you a post office address. A letter will be a conversation medium between us. We will write letters within one month. Whenever I will come home; we will meet at the school campus.

Ok! That's a great idea; I said.

She reached her home. Her father held one stick; he started beating her without any question. She was crying in front of her mother. Mothering of mother forced to save her daughter. Her mother took her in the arms.

Why did you meet with Ankit? Her father asked.

She looked towards her mother and said; Mom, I did not go with him. I went with my friend Sarita. Ankit met me at the Deepawali festival with his parents. I did not have any communication with him.

Anjali, come here; he called her.

Yes, papa.

You just get ready. I will drop you at your Nanihal.

She had spent only a few days with her mother and all families' members. She was trying to convince him but he did not agree.

She got ready; she was crying because she wanted to spend her full vacation with her mother. Finally, her father dropped her at Nanihal.

Her parents started looking for a bridegroom for her. He discussed it with all members of the family. Everyone was agreed to get her married but they did not tell her their decision.

CHAPTER THREE

Letters

She persuaded her 10+2. Finally, she came home. She met with a few guests who wanted to see her. She introduced her to them. They asked about her education and home chores nothing else.

She replied that she wanted to continue her studies; she completed her intermediate. She did not want to get married until she will be graduated but her father has to get married soon.

The next day, she met me and talked about guests. I did not know what to do. It seemed to me that I was losing a precious thing from life. My heart was breathing hard, and I could not control myself. I took a rest in her arm; she was scared that someone might see us and informed her parent.

Ankit, I don't want to get married to someone else except you. You and I will never leave each other coz our soul's blossom lake a Lilly of the valley.

We met with Sarita because those guests came from her relatives. She knew that boy who was getting married to Anjali. He was from her aunt's village.

I gave responsibility to her friend Sarita that she can tell him about our relationship.

She requested her father that she wanted to visit her aunt's home because she wished to meet with her aunt. Her father dropped her at her aunt's home.

She inquired about that boy with the help of her cousin. She met with the boy and told him about Anjali and Ankit. He was a good person and have sensible humor. He agreed that he will not get married to Anjali.

He talked with his father that he wanted to continue his studies, so he will not get married very soon. Her father forced him but he was determined. He went to Anjali's home with his parents. He directly met her father who was cleaning his van.

Namaskar uncle.

Yes, beta, what happened?

Uncle, I will not get married very soon coz I want to further study.

He was astonished because Sumit directly decided that he will not get married to her daughter. She was cleaning her wardrobe. Sumit fall in love with her for a few moments but he controlled his emotion.

Everyone was getting worried about her marriage. They were worried about rejection. His family agreed but it was a sudden rejection by him.

Sarita told us that he decided that he will not get married to Anjali. This news was a medicine for my unpleasant pain. Anjali was flying in the sky. It was not possible to meet again if he did not deny getting married to her.

CHAPTER FOUR

Adulthood

I pursued my graduation from my hometown college. I studied hard because my parents wanted to see me as a police officer, and Anjali was one of my backbones who always supported me financially and mentally.

She was pursuing her graduation from Lucknow University. We spent our valuable moments at the coffee shop. We completely fell in love with each other. We knew that without love nothing will exist on this planet. Our romance period had been started. We decided that we will be life partners forever.

I was preparing for the police officer's entrance exam at home. I was belonging to a very rural area where no electricity was available so I used to light a lantern for study at night. We used the fire of woods for cooking.

We pursued our graduation. Now, we were aspiring to become whatever we wanted to become. Anjali wrote the teacher's entrance exam. I also wrote the UPSC exam but I did not have too much background knowledge about the syllabus and subjects of UPSC. But we were waiting for the result. She knew that she will crack the exam but I was not sure about my result.

She cracked the exam and was selected for the school teacher. We were thrilled and celebrated her achievement.

Her dry eyes were irrigated by hope. She was an independent girl. She decided that she will not get married for two years.

I was failed my first attempt exam. It was my first failure in my life. I was isolated for a few days and cried alone in the corner of the room. I touched the taste of failure, which was very bitter. I went home and sat on the cot. I was distraught. I did not want to tell them my failure who wanted to see me as a police officer. I was thinking that if they will listen that I failed to clear the UPSC exam then they will get heartbreak, so I kept silent.

I saw my parents were working on the farm. I could not say that I will join coaching classes. I could not say that I did not clear the UPSC exam. My mother sold her jewelry for my education. I wanted to tell them that I was unable to clear the UPSC exam but I have had no courage to share my failure with my beloved parents.

I could not share it with anyone but I need to share it with someone special in my life. I called her; she came with a few snacks. Firstly, she opened a packet of samosa.

Ankit, please, take it; she offered me.

I took one piece of samosa and started eating. She was telling me about her day. What did she teach students and how did she spend her day? I was listening to everything. Sometimes, I passed fake smiles.

Ankit, why are you so upset?; she asked.

I could not reply.

I saw her charming and glowing face. Her smile was spreading a light, which was coming on my sad face. Her eyes were skipping something. She accepted that I will share my failure with her but I did not.

Ankit, could you see your result? She asked.

I did not reply to a single word.

She kissed me and said; my dear, I had seen your result but you have to need more practice. You should join coaching classes to compete with all competitors.

Anjali, you know well that my parents cannot bear my study, so I cannot join any classes.

Don't worry dear, I am a working girl. I will bear your all expenses. You go to Allahabad, where many students are preparing for this toughest exam. You will get ideas about questions and will learn from experienced teachers.

What about your father if he will ask for your money?

Don't worry dear; I will manage it.

She giggled and held my hand. She encouraged and motivated me for my next journey. She boosted me as fuel works for running an engine.

Ankit, can I ask something?

Yes, I replied.

Although it is not your dream, you want to be a police officer. You should be clear in your mind that why should you want to write this exam. And you should never forget your heart's voice.

Yes, this is true that I never discussed my passions with you. It's a good time to share with you. I want to become a police officer, which is my parent's dream but my passions are different apart from this but anywhere every passion has a strong connection with my dreams. I want to touch the horizon of the sky but my feet will be on the earth.

Anjali, who will take care of my parents?

Don't worry because they are my future mother-in-law and father-in-law. I will take care of them, and we will get medicine tomorrow. You have to need to come with them at sharp 4 PM to my school. We will get their treatment from a good doctor.

Ok, Dear, I replied.

The next day, I visited the hospital with my parents and Anjali. The doctor started treatment of them. He was performing a lot of testing. We spent more than one hour in the hospital.

Beti, you are paying for medicine. It is not good. I will give you my gold ring, which I have been keeping for our daughter in law; my mother said.

No worries mom, I am part of your family; I am your daughter-in-law; she giggles.

Beti, how will it happen coz we don't have the same level. Your parent will punish you if they will know that you are going to marry my son.

Do not worry, uncle. I will handle it.

My parents were getting better day by day. They were happy that she was my friend.

CHAPTER FIVE

Allahabad

I was ready to go to Allahabad. I did not want to leave my parents alone but I read a quote *"Hard work and sacrifices are the keys to success"*.

Anjali dropped me at the bus stop. She kissed me and told me that Ankit you have the potential to clear this toughest exam. I could not keep my promise but I decided that I will clear this toughest exam within one year. I missed my home, my parents, and my beloved Anjali. I reached Allahabad at midnight.

I always thought that if I will not clear this exam within one year then what will answer my parent and Anjali. These things were motivated me. It had kept me isolated and cut off from all types of distractions.

I used to talk with my parents within two weeks and come home in every harvesting. I used to do farming every season. I used to talk with Anjali once a week.

I revised all the topics. UPSC exam, which was my second attempt. I have had faith that I will clear this exam. I cleared the written exam. She was thrilled when I shared this good news with her.

Ankit, you should focus on your interview. You will clear it easily.

Yes, Anjali, I will do my best.

Her father was looking for a bridegroom. He visited her aunt's home where he met with a person. He decided that Anjali will get married to him. He opted for the first meeting with the bridegroom's parents. She met with his parents and relatives who came to her home. She worried about our relationship but she could not utter any word in front of her parent or family. The priest had decided wedding date. Her father booked a marriage hall. He sent an invitation to his relatives.

Someone told me that Anjali will get married very soon. She was crying every day. She was not talking with anyone. My blood was boiling at a hundred degrees Celsius temperature when I heard it. I ran towards her home. It took around 15 minutes to reach her home. I saw she was washing clothes. I asked for her wedding date. She did not say anything except cry.

Where is everyone? I asked.

They went to the market for my wedding shopping.

What? I surprised.

Could you tell him about our relationship? I asked with shivering lips.

Yes,

What did they say?

They are not agreed.

No, yaar I will talk to your father. If he will kill me then I will die for you.

Ankit, go away please; I love you that's why I am saying. It is not a safe moment for us. I am waiting for your interview result. You just need to focus on your interview. You have only one month.

What date of your marriage? I asked furiously.

I have only 15 days to get married but do not worry dear, I am only for you, and want to see you as an IAS.

Anjali, I will tell your parents that I love you.

No, Ankit. You have sworn that you don't have any conversation with my family members related to my marriage or love relationship. If you love me then you will not try to get a conversation with my parents or family members; Anjali said.

Ok, Anjali, but I will not live without you. We will get married very soon.

Ankit, you just clear your interview and we get married very soon; she said.

She dropped me at the bus station. She told me that Ankit, you should focus on your interview, which is important for you.

What about your marriage? How will I stop it? I asked.

Do not worry. I will handle it. You just concentrate on your target. I will leave the universe instead of getting married to someone else.

What are you saying, Anjali? This statement scared me.

Tears were pouring from her eyes; she did not want to leave me.

Ankit, I love you, you are everything to me. I cannot go with someone else. I cannot live without you. I will meet in the reincarnation if I die.

Anjali doesn't tell like this. We will get married soon.

I saw her eyes were wet; she wanted to say something. She was hiding something inside her heart. She was scared to lose me. I did not want to leave her alone and I did not want to break her hope. So, I left my fairy and love.

After one week, she called me for a sudden meeting. I came from Allahabad and met with her. She registered as a nominee in her bank account.

Anjali, why are you doing it?

Ankit, it means you can withdraw money from my account when I will die early than you. I have mentioned here my and your relationship as a spouse.

No, Anju, sometimes I called her nickname. I will die together; I said.

Ankit, it is not possible that we will die on the same day and same time because people do not get birth at the same time, I cannot see my destiny. I have already achieved my dream. I have one dream, which will take time to achieve. I cannot tell you right now because that is a secret for you. I will give you a surprise; She said.

It was time to get her married. Everyone was happy except her. She was dying day by day but could not say it with anyone even with me. Every relative was coming at her marriage. Her father sent an invitation to every relative and neighbor. A few came before the wedding date and a few came on the same date.

Every ritual was performed for a successful marriage. A wedding's possession came in the evening. People were dancing. They quenched their thirst. They also finished dinner.

She was ready for going into the marriage hall. She went with her to the marriage hall, where the bridegroom, bridegroom's family, and her family were sitting. The priest was chanting mantras; she was taking round around fire. She completed only one round and fell on the earth. Her body had been cold. She was not saying anything. White foam was coming from her mouth. Her face was black and her body was getting cold. Her condition was critical. She could not speak, could not walk, and could not see anyone.

Her bridegroom left her. He did not take her hospital. He did not want to get married to a patient. Everyone left her home instead of a few relatives who took her to the hospital.

I attended the interview, which was the final round of the UPSC exam. I qualified to interview. I was thrilled and wanted to tell my dear Anjali. I dialed her college landline number and asked about Anjali. Her colleague told me that she was getting married. She was on the leave for one month. She gave me a few photocopies, letters, and bank paper. You should come here, and collect it.

CHAPTER SIX

Hospital

I was sure that something was not happening well with her because she already told me a few words, which were making me worry. I boarded a bus from the Allahabad bus stand and reached home. I met with her colleague and asked about Anjali. She was crying in front of me without saying anything.

I am scared, where is she? I want to meet her; her silence was killing me.

She was admitted to ICU and wanted to meet you. She has swollen an excess amount of poison; she replied emotionally.

Could you take me to the hospital, please; I requested.

Why not; she replied.

We went to the hospital using public transport. I saw her parents were crying. I thought they would not allow me to meet her, but they did not disallow me. I bowed to her parents. Her father blessed me with wet eyes.

Finally, I met with my beloved who was living a critical life. Her body was black, and she was bedridden for one week.

Anjali, why did you do it? Why did you try to leave me alone in this universe? How did you think that I will live in this world without you?

I cannot leave without you, Ankit. My father told me that he will commit suicide if I will get married to you. Therefore, I agreed to get married to someone else.

I never told you because I knew if I get married to someone else then I will feel regret forever and you will not live a happy life. If I will leave this universe then you cry for a few days and will forget me at last.

How was your final interview? She was excited to know the result.

I cleared the interview and became an IAS officer. My training will start within a few days.

Did you not go home? She asked.

No, I just directly come here.

Ankit, you should distribute sweets in the hospital because you achieved your biggest dreams. I bought sweets from the market and distributed them to the hospital. Everyone congratulated me. I was feeling proud of my Anjali, who always supported me. I gave all credit to my parents and Anjali.

I saw her parents were standing behind me, they heard our conversation. Their draining eyes were saying something. They called me and offered me a vacant place beside them.

I am sorry, please forgive me. I could not understand your true love.

You can stay with her. She has to need you.

No, uncle, I will not stay here alone because she loves you more than me that's why she did not disrespect you.

Her parents started crying and kissed her daughter. They hugged each other. They said; dear daughter you will get well soon because you will get married to Ankit. She heard it from her parents; she got down from the bed and started moving towards her parents. Her parent was ecstatic. I could not control my emotions, which were flowing inside my veins and heart. I hugged her for five minutes and kissed them on her forehead.

CHAPTER SEVEN

End of Life

We stayed in the hospital for two days. The doctor discharged her. I told my parents that I want to be an IAS officer. I said that I am getting married to Anjali. Tears of happiness poured from their eyes.

I got married to Anjali. It was my new journey. I gave all facilities to my parents. She lived with my parents.

We went on a trip. We were enjoying our married life. We visited our favorite places. My parents also enjoyed their life. We were an ecstatic couple on this planet.

We all were going on the occasion of the wedding of my friend. I was driving the car. Suddenly, a tunnel came into the road, I tried to control the car but it was not possible due to the failure of the break. We got an accident in the flu-flung area. My car braked down and tumbled on the big hill. Everyone got deep injuries and was helpless. I could not able to hear the last voice of my parents who instantly died. Blood was pouring from the floor of the car. I saw, Anjali was breathing slowly, she wanted to help me but we could not help each other. We were crawling due to high pain. We could not walk because we are far away from the road. I was living in this world for you. I am going to leave you and will meet you in reincarnation. She held me tightly in her arms, kissed me, and left her body.

This was the biggest grief in my life that I could not see it. I was looking that my whole family was passing in front of me and I was unable to save them. Blood was pouring from my head. I was not able to breathe. I knew that my soul wanted to leave my body. Anjali, I am also coming. We will meet again. I will wait for you....

CHAPTER EIGHT

Reincarnation

My reincarnation revives my memories and beloved. My eyes are thirsty for her. I don't know when and how we will meet each other but I thank God for this precious and valuable life.

Anjali is my true love of reincarnation. I never forget her, and her support. She loves me and makes me a unique person in my life.

My beloved ♥?♥?Anjali. I have been waiting............